You Can do whatever you want to
do, when you

Potential

I he _Real_ -U- Empowered

# The Heartbeat of Madness
## Daniel G. Cullen

June 3. 2018

PublishAmerica
Baltimore

First printing

All characters in this book are fictitious, and any resemblance to real persons, living or dead, is coincidental.

ISBN: 1-4241-8167-4
PUBLISHED BY PUBLISHAMERICA, LLLP
www.publishamerica.com
Baltimore

Printed in the United States of America

# JOURNEY INTO DARKNESS

Twenty-five years is a long time, especially when you consider it as a prison sentence. It is nine thousand, one hundred and twenty-five days and nights. I spent every one of those days and nights locked in solitary confinement. My prison cell was a mental one of anger and rage. The guards who kept me confined were named Guilt and Shame.

Guilt told me I had done wrong, and Shame told me I was wrong. I never came out of this inner prison and no one ever came in. Alone, I cried so many tears, until I realized no one heard me. I slipped into a deeper madness. I was lost in a deeper darkness, alone.

In a country full of people, I shuffled from the West Coast to the East Coast. I have lost count of the curbsides where I have sat. Faces became a blur and voices were just a hum. I was a statistic, a number on a piece of paper, a homeless man. Twenty-five years living on the street, walking as a dead man on two feet.

# Walking Dead Man

When I was sixteen, I started to roam, leaving home
To be on my own, From Kelowna to Kenora, from
Rue Saint Louie to Grande Prairie, I have seen this
Country, the True North strong and free, I love it for
What it is, home to my family and me. But I was done
Wrong and through madness I have gone.
I was not done
Wrong by the land from sea to sea but by a deviant
Who made my Soul bleed.
It was not a gun or a knife that
Took the spirit of my life;
It was a man who liked his boys
Cute and nice,
He raped me, robbed me, and left me to die.
Now,
My words make you wonder, you may even shake
Your head, but there is more to this story there is more
To be said,
On a dark and lonely highway I died and lost my soul, but
All around this country
A walking dead man people got to
Know.
Deep festering rot of guilt
And shame, these two emotions I
Will call them pain.
From which I could not run on foot, bus, or plane.
With these two emotions I walked and a life I feigned.
From Victoria to Charlotte Town
I looked for life but it was
Never found. So I drowned in a bottle.
Drugs numbed me.
Deeper and deeper the grave was dug.

People pointed
And called
Me a thug, I can give the hobos a tour
Of all the fine lodgings
And exquisite cuisine ditches
And dumpsters, places I have
Been, seen.
Mental and emotional hiding places
Are all well known me,
Wherever I went, there I would be.
It drove me to madness. I was never free.
Hiding from you, hiding from me; all because a devi-
ant Fulfilled his perversions on me.
Nothing tormented me more than to think
I would not be free.
The purveyors of mental health are the most vicious
And mean. They gave
Me twenty-two names but I will give me one;
I will call me insane.
Pills, jails and institutions, I came so close to death,
All because a deviant
Fulfilled his lust. He liked his boys cute and nice
with no hair on their chest.
Twenty-five years of guilt and shame, a festering rot
Of emotional pain.
Now my words may make you wonder you may even
Shake your head but
This is my story alive from the dead.

It was nineteen seventy-four in Kelowna, British Columbia. We lived in a five bedroom house. My father was a popular radio personality. My mother was a real estate agent. Two of my brothers and sisters also lived at home. We lived in a middle-class neighborhood. Our house was on Wasilow Road. I really loved this house. The front yard had lush green grass. I loved to walk with bare feet and feel the cool grass on the bottom of my feet, and to play with Josh our dog, a mutt, who loved to walk around with a rock in his mouth. He would drop the rock at your feet. His game was to try and stop you from picking it up, and when you did finally pick it up, he would bark and jump until you threw the rock, then would chase after it, only to bring it back and start all over again.

I was twelve years old. Our family had moved to Kelowna from Fort Saint John. My parents had bought property and built the house from the foundation. There was an open field behind the house that led back to a large hill that I loved to climb; at the top of the hill there was still more open land. I roamed those hills alone and with my friends for hours during the summers. When I wasn't on some adventure I would be at Sarson's beach swimming. I was growing up in a good home, with awesome parents, who both had careers.

Kelowna in the '70s was a town of about seventy thousand people, located along the shores of Lake Okanogan. The lake stretched eighty miles from north to south, in a valley with the same name, located in central British Columbia.

My father and I used to go to hockey games in the wintertime. As sports director of one of the local radio stations it was his responsibility to report on these hockey games. I loved going with him. We would sit in the press box that overlooked the rink; it was the best seat in the house. I was in awe of my father. He had worked hard and everyone knew Frank. I was referred to by people as Frank's son, a title I was always proud of. In the summer time we would go to men's fast ball. One time our seat was in the press box behind home plate at King's Stadium.

My mother was the glue that held the family together. She stands only five feet tall but her inner stature made her a giant. She always told me, "Quitters don't win and winners don't quit." She has always had a very profound faith. She instilled in me my early roots for the faith I hold so dear in my heart today. I always enjoyed it when we would be coming home from somewhere and she would pull into the local Dairy Queen and we would be treated to a milkshake. On hot summer days she would buy cold meats from the local butcher and buns from the bakery and would make the most incredible sandwiches. When she made her chili I would eat until I felt like my stomach would explode.

When I was fifteen I met a man whose name was Bob. We met at the Kelowna General Hospital where he lived. He was a big man confined to a wheelchair because of muscular dystrophy. I worked once a week at the hospital on his ward and every week I would feed him. We would have great conversations, and I always looked forward to seeing him. When I take the time, almost thirty years later, to think of how humble he was, I really could see that he was a great man in his heart. As big and as young as he was, he gracefully allowed a fifteen-year-old boy to feed him, and made me feel as good as I did. I am honored to have met him. He told me what he was like before he got sick. He was a man you would not have wanted as an enemy. Now his disease had confined him to a wheelchair with someone feeding him. In spite of this, he was a calm, peaceful man.

One day he started to tell me why: he had this thing he called faith. He told me the story of Jesus and what He was to him. "That's why I am who I am," he would say. Bob had a calm peaceful approach to life.

One day Bob asked me how to spell my name. I told him and he thanked me. That was it; soon it got busy on the ward and I forgot all about it. At the end of my shift I went home, but first I said good-bye to my friend. Next week when I came to work, he was all excited to see me, he told me he had a gift for me. "Come and see me when you are not busy," he said. It was about an hour before I got a chance to see him again. When I did, he said, "Let's go into the side room."

When we were there, with a big smile on his face, he pulled out a blue leather bound King James Bible with my name embossed on the front of it. I did not know what to say, but my parents had taught me manners, so I said, "Thank you."

At the age of fifteen, I started reading the Bible and I have never been without one since. I have carried one with me through all my travels. I have read it countless times over the years.

My twin sister is a very smart woman. She always excelled in learning. It started when she was young and it has never stopped. In grade two she passed on to grade three and I did not. I seemed to be a slower learner and so the school kept me back to repeat grade two. It was not my parents' fault, neither was it my twin sister's fault, but the comment was always: "Why can't you be like Betty?"

I was getting a sense of who I was as a person, my sense of self was very low. Looking back more than thirty years, I clearly see I was struggling to find self-acceptance and a sense of who I was as a person. I knew my name was Nobody but who was I? How did I define myself? I didn't. I gravitated to trouble.

To me that was when I was noticed the most. So I stole a gun one day, from the closet of my friend's house. It was his father's gun. He had hidden it in the bedroom closet. My friend had shown it to me on several occasions. When we were in his house alone, my friend went to the washroom and I went into his father's closet to where the gun was and I stole it. I quickly hid it under my shirt and made an excuse to go home. When I got home I hid the gun in my room; but first I wanted to play with it. I was amazed how it felt, the weight, the coldness of the steel. I felt a sense of self-worth, I had a gun.

In nineteen seventy-four metal detectors were not the norm in middle-class neighborhood schools; especially in a small town of less then one hundred thousand people. I did not have any problem taking the gun into the school. It was under my shirt stuffed into the waist of my pants. I walked the halls with a new sense of importance. This feeling went to my head and I was infected with a disease I call Big-shot-iteis. The symptoms are: your head gets swollen, your mouth opens wide, and your tongue becomes loose. I started to brag and it did not take long for the principal to hear about there being a gun in his school and he made me open my locker to inspect the contents of it. When he did, there was the gun. The gun was confiscated and I was taken to the office.

My mind raced as I developed a story of how I came to have a gun. I told my contrived story. I explained how I was walking to school and along the way I was kicking an empty pop can down the road. It went into the weeds along the side of the road. I went to get it. I told him I found the gun. The principal bought my story. He sent me back to class. I spent the rest of the day troubled over what was going to happen when school was over.

When I walked out the front door of the school my father was waiting for me. He drove me home: a neighbor who was a police officer wanted to talk to me. He wanted to ask me some questions about the gun. I told him the same story I had told to the principal earlier that day. He thanked me and then he left.

In my own mind, I thought I had gotten away with it. Every thing was okay for about two days, then on the third day as I walked into the house after school, my mother yelled my name.

"Nobody!" There was a tone I was familiar with and I knew I was in trouble. She confronted me: "You stole the gun, didn't you?" She did not wait for an answer. She launched into a lecture and she lectured me for about half an hour. She was furious. With an exasperated breath she sent me to my room and told me to stay there until my father got home.

My heart raced faster with each passing minute. I paced in my room. As much as I loved my father I also feared him. He was not an abusive father but he was a father who believed in discipline. A flash came across my mind. "Run away" was the idea, so I did. I climbed out the basement window and ran up into the hills that surrounded our neighborhood. After about three hours wandering the hills, I found a spot where I could see my house from a distance and I watched as my mother paced in front of the window. She paced for hours. I can only now understand the pain I was causing her; one of her twins was missing.

I came home about midnight. I was expecting to be in a lot of trouble. I was tired and hungry so I came home. The trouble that I thought I was in never materialized. My parents were just relieved that I was safe at home. I had never run away before so after a hug from my mother and a few words from my father, I went to bed. Although the experience was over, a seed had been planted that would follow me for thirty years. My philosophy was whenever I am in trouble or scared, run.

This was the birth of my life on the streets as a runaway. Running away became a frustrating pattern for my parents. On one occasion when I ran away, I discovered LSD (lysergic acid diethyl amid). LSD is known as "Acid" with brand names such as Purple Microdot, Window Pain or Green Blotter. Each dose is called a hit. My introduction to street drugs that day was two double hits of Green Blotter and one single hit of Acid, the equivalent of five hits of Acid at one time. On that day I exploded into my drug habit. Now being a runaway had new meaning, drugs. I also started to break into cars, businesses and houses to steal anything that I liked. I was a juvenile delinquent with a drug addiction.

In nineteen seventy-eight my mother and father went on a vacation without me, or my brothers and sisters. They left us with a babysitter. I was sixteen and I had my driver's license. My mother left her car at home. It was a green four-door station wagon, and they took my father's car; a recipe for trouble. There were two other guys, a girl, and myself and on the spur of the moment we decided to take the car and leave town. (Steal it.)

For the next three days, we drove to the West Coast. All the way there we broke into houses and stole gas. When we got to Hope, B.C., we had enough liquor to have a party. I started to drink lemon gin. When I had drunk enough to be slobbering drunk I decided to go swim in the Fraser River. My friends finally got me out of the river. They locked me in the back of the station wagon where I promptly passed out. When I finally gained consciousness I was on the ferry going to Vancouver Island.

We made our way to Gold Stream Park. It was here that we were surrounded by the police and placed under arrest. After we were busted, I was sent to a receiving home, and my father was contacted. When he came to get me, I told him I did not want to go home. He told me very clearly that I was to get into the car. The drive back to Kelowna was extremely quiet and tense. When we arrived home, I ran away again the very next day.

Drugs, alcohol and crime were now fueling my sense of self-worth. I was found in Calgary, Alberta. When my father found me this time, his words to me were: "If you want to be on your own, you are on your own." On that note he shook my hand and said, "Good luck."

Years later, I learned that my parents had decided that if I was arrested, they would tell the authorities to keep me. They would go to Children's Aid and say, "Give him a new home. We don't want him." I do not blame my parents for doing this. I had left them with no choice. I had exasperated the patience of two great people.

"The journey of a thousand miles begins beneath one's feet." —Lao Tuze

When my journey across Canada started, I was a juvenile delinquent. The thing that made it even worse was that I had no sense of self-identity or self-worth. Hindsight has taught me this. But in nineteen seventy-eight I was king of the road. I was free to go wherever I wanted, whenever I wanted to go. When I left Calgary, I headed east. That is all I had in mind, going east.

My first stop was in Winnipeg, Manitoba. I can never forget Portage and Main. The wind at that intersection has a reputation that blows from coast to coast. It was here I met a girl. Her name has gone from my mind, but I remember that my sixteen-year-old heart skipped a beat. It picked up its pace as soon as I saw her. One word to describe her is "wow." All I wanted to do was impress her. My testosterone kicked in and common sense kicked out. We talked for a long time. When she learned I had no place to sleep, she invited me to her place. Now my mind went numb with imaginary anticipation. She shared a home with a couple of other people. In the middle of Canada, with people I did not know, I started to drink.

That night I was determined to do one thing, impress my newfound female desire. As the beers entered into my bloodstream and my head started to get lighter, the funniest thing happened; I got a syndrome that happened every time I got drunk. I started to feel ten feet tall and bulletproof. I felt invincible. I had liquid courage. The conversation turned to the tattoos. My mouth opened wide and my talk was big. One of the people turned and said, "I'll give you a tattoo." My words had cast the die. I had no choice, if I was going to impress this girl. He took an arrowhead medallion (popular in the '70s) that he had on a chain around his neck. He took my left wrist and traced the medallion onto it. He took a sewing needle, tied thread around the tip so that the needle would not go too far into my arm, and proceeded to dip the pin into the Indian ink. For three hours he poked the pin into my wrist. When he was finished, I was the proud owner of a new tattoo. The girl I so desperately wanted to impress? She went to bed with her boyfriend. The next day when I got up, my wrist was still swollen and my head ached. I had a hangover in a real bad way and my ego was deflated.

I moved into the single men's hostel in downtown Winnipeg. This would be my second stay in a place that for the next twenty-five years would be my home. Whatever city I found myself in, if there was a shelter there I would stay there.

While I was in the Winnipeg shelter, I met a man, who was about forty-five to fifty years of age. He saw an opportunity; a young looking boy, who looked innocent. He came and talked with me and said, "I have this full proof plan to make money. It's called rehashing, it works like this. I will shoplift clothes from one store that will fit you. Then we will go to another store and you give a story how your grandma got you this gift for your birthday, but this one doesn't fit you. You get the money back for it and give it to me, and I will split it with you. This lasted for about a month. I quickly got bored, and left Winnipeg.

I hitchhiked to Quebec City, where I stayed with one of

my older sisters. She had an apartment on rue Saint Louie. It was located in the old Quebec City across the street from an old tree that had grown around a cannon ball. The canon ball had been there since the 1800s and the tree had grown around it. My sister's apartment was above a gift shop. I was just a few blocks away from the historic hotel where I would walk along the boardwalk, or I would wander the narrow streets of old Quebec. Of all the cities and towns, I have seen in twenty-five years, my fondest memory is of the time when I was with my sister in Quebec City. I stayed at my sister's apartment for about one and a half months until she bought me a one-way greyhound bus ticket back to British Columbia. I was always looking for ways to have money in my pocket, so in the next town, after I left Quebec City, I traded the one-way ticket in for the remaining cash and started to hitchhike my way to the West Coast. After six months of being on my own, I was starting to realize I did not want to be on my own. Home was starting to look not so bad. I realized my parents' rules were a good thing, and I was getting sick of being drunk or stoned. That had lost their flavor more than I wanted to admit.

As I was traveling back west from Quebec, I had a real sense of aloneness; it is so much worse than being lonely. For three thousand miles, aloneness traveled with me, I wanted to change. I wanted to go home. I wanted a home cooked meal. I wanted my own bed. I wanted my family. I did not want to do drugs anymore. That's when Bob came to mind. His peace is what I wanted. He told me many times that his peace came from his faith. I wanted that peace.

The Bible that Bob had given me was just a trophy book. It did not have the meaning to me that it does today. I started to think about what I had learned about the story that was found in the pages of that book. The journey back west became very difficult. The more I started to see the condition I was in the less I slept and the more disheveled I became. Someone had told me there was a place where I could find help for my addiction and a place that would teach me about the faith I was looking for. They said the name of the place; it was a homeless shelter. I do not know how I ended up in Grande Prairie, Alberta, but I did.

Over the many times I have traveled across Canada I have always enjoyed coming into a city after spending days on the road. To me it is a rush of emotion to watch the city appear in the distance. When you come into Grande Prairie, the horizon is flat. For miles, you see what appears to be a black dot. The closer you get the bigger the dot gets until its identity presents itself. It is the one office tower in the city. When I got there, I was tired and hungry but that all changed when I realized that there was a place to lodge; a shelter for single men run by a Christian organization that had an addiction rehab program. It was the fall of 1978 and I was ready to change. With a sense of anticipation, I entered the doors but this was not to be the beginning of the end of my drug addiction and my short life on the streets. It was only the end of the beginning of a twenty-five year sentence.

# A DARK AND LONELY HIGHWAY

The writing of this chapter for me was not easy, neither was it pleasurable, but it was necessary. The telling of this experience for me has been a very therapeutic undertaking. For twenty-five years I felt vile and useless. As I took the time to write, it became very clear to me why I felt the way I did. I have healed in my own heart and mind enough to come to the place of writing this chapter. The process has still been very hard but it was even more of a healing.

There is a question in a report on homelessness, written by the Parliamentary Research Branch in Ottawa that asked, "What are the variables that force people to the ranks of homelessness?" The report goes to say that there are as many reasons as there are homeless people. The conclusion to the question is correct; everyone who has lived on the streets has their own reason for being there. In my research I have come to understand, that one in three girls in Canada is sexually assaulted before the age of eighteen. That is almost eleven million girls. I have also come to understand that one in six boys before the age of eighteen is sexually assaulted. That is almost six million boys. I am one of those six million boys. There is one more statistic that I want to bring to your attention. It is estimated that almost five hundred thousand people are homeless in Canada, and eighty percent of those people suffer from some sort of mental disorder, that is four hundred thousand people. I was one of those four hundred thousand people. I think it is only prudent that as a writer I warn you, the reader, that what you are going to read may disturb you. But please remember that every one, man or woman, who has been sexually assaulted has had to come to terms with their own experience of being assaulted and realize they are not to be blamed.

# OUR SECRET...

I had traveled for several days prior to reaching Grande Prairie. I was tired and dirty. I had only taken short naps in the passenger seat of those who had picked me up as I hitchhiked from Quebec. I learned early in my hitchhiking days that when you are picked up from the side of the highway that you're expected to keep the driver awake. How do you do that? You learn to listen and ask questions at the right time. The more personable you are, the friendlier the driver becomes. It makes the ride easier for both of you.

I only weighed about one hundred pounds and my hair was shoulder length. I still had not started to shave. I looked like a child. People asked me what I was doing. Why wasn't I at home or in school? I would just respond, "I got kicked out of the house." It would stop the questions, but it did not always stop the advice. Another word for that advice would be lecture.

When I finally made it to town, I found my way to the

welfare office. They told me about a homeless shelter and gave me instructions on how to find the place. I found it on a street that was close to the local hospital, next to a retirement home, and across the street from a junior high school. Sitting back from the street about fifty feet, the property was well groomed. To me it looked like an oasis for my weary body. When I walked through the front door, I noticed the floor was tiled with red square tiles. I went up the first three steps. The man behind the desk looked at me from behind a glass as he sat in his office. He pointed to the door at the top of the next three steps. I went through that door and was standing between two doors. It was a kind of security system for the building. To my right there was another window.

"May I help you?" the man behind the glass asked me. I looked at him. He stood about five feet nine inches tall, his hair was thick, jet-black and wavy. He had black-framed glasses that reminded me of the ones my father wore. The man wore a crisp white shirt with two blue shoulder bars and he had a pair of dark blue pants on. He looked like a soldier in uniform.

I smiled and said, "I was sent here by Social Services. They said I could find a place to sleep."

He said, "Come in." The door in front of me started to buzz. "Wait in the lobby. I will be with you in a moment."

I walked through the door and was immediately impressed by how clean the place was and how clean it smelled. Unlike the shelter in Calgary, Alberta, or the one in Winnipeg, it felt safe. In reality I was a lamb in a wolf's den. I was standing in front of the Coke machine, when I heard a voice behind me say, "Sorry to keep you waiting." I turned to see who was talking to me. It was the man that had been behind the window. He was standing in front of me. He stuck out his right hand and said, "My name is Jack. I am the shelter manager." It will only take about twenty minutes to register you, then I will give you a tour."

This process took about forty-five minutes. Jack presented himself as a nice man. He listened. He seemed to genuinely care. After days of travel I was finally starting to unwind but this was a bad mistake. Being so young and naïve I did not know any better but Jack was very cunning and diabolical. At the end of the tour he showed me the lounge. When he left the room, I sat on the couch and immediately fell asleep. I woke up by a shaking of my shoulder. With a smile on his face, he chuckled and said, "You are going to miss supper."

I jumped up. I was starving. As I walked into the dining room most of the men had already eaten their food and the room was almost empty. I got my food and Jack came and sat with me. Jack was taking the time with me to find out who I was and why was I living in a shelter. I told him I had left home and been across Canada. A smile grew on his face. Back then, I thought it was because he was impressed that I had gone across Canada on my own. He said, "You have seen a lot for being so young." He took me under his wing, so to speak.

Over the next several days I told him I really wanted to quit drinking and doing drugs. He told me that they had a ninety-day rehab program that was based on the Bible. That made me feel a hope that maybe I could find the peace I saw in Bob's eyes. We talked about God. I showed him the Bible that Bob had given me. It was my one treasured possession. I was awed by the story, as I still am today. Jack told me things about God. I was really becoming comfortable with Jack. He was helping me feel that maybe I could move home, when my parents saw that I had made changes in my life.

One day Jack said, "If you want a more peaceful place to relax, you can sit in my room when I am on shift."

He lived on the premises on the first floor. The room

had a bed close to the window that faced the front of the building. There was a table with two chairs and a brown lazy boy chair. I often sat in the chair and fell asleep. One time I opened my eyes and saw Jack staring at me.

He said, "Sorry to wake you, I just came to get something. I want to talk to you after I am off my shift."

"No problem," I said as he turned and walked out of the room.

He came in about ten o'clock. We talked until about eleven that night. All of a sudden the questions became very personal.

"Are you a virgin?" he asked.

I blushed and replied, "Yes."

He looked at me with a smile. It was warm and assuring. He asked if I had ever seen a naked girl. He asked me a lot of questions about my sexuality. His questions were doing two things: arousing my lust, and confusing my mind. I was asking myself why he was asking me these questions. I was feeling weird in my gut. Then Jack told me, "God made these feelings so we can express them to another person. God has also made some men, with the desire to love another man." (I was not a man I was a boy. There was almost twenty years between us). He looked at me straight in the eye and said, "Have you ever had feelings for another man?"

My heart felt like it skipped a beat; my mind started to race faster. He reached over and kissed me on the lips. Fear filled my heart and my head swirled with confusion, I think Jack sensed that and said, "Sorry if I startled you. I think you should go to bed. We will talk tomorrow." Before I left he said, "Just keep this between us." I said nothing but nodded my head to indicate yes.

# STAND WITH ME

As I leave a city. Any city it does not matter.
I walk with the flow of traffic to the edge of
That city place my bags beside
Me on the edge of the highway,
Stand with me as
My back is to the future and my face is to
The past,
Stand with me
As I extend my right thumb in the
Direction of the Traffic I am on a ribbon of pain.
For twenty-five years I traveled the Trans-Canada
Highway fueled by anger and rage:
I really do understand Hate. Death does not scare me:
I have stood at death's door four times
Stand with me
As I travel with one incessant thought
That will not leave me alone, "Why
Did you do that to me?" I hate myself.
I hate you
Stand with me
On the highway, with my back to the future
And my face to the past
Stand with me.

This was the mindset that drove me as I started my life as a homeless man. A transient, traveling along moving farther and farther away from society. When I left that homeless shelter I hitchhiked to Fort Saint John British, Columbia.

In every town I found myself in, it did not matter, I would find myself going to church. I would find a phone book and go to the yellow pages under church. I would look for a church that interested me and I would go to it. As ironic as it might sound, I was still looking for the God that Bob told me about. At the same time I wanted to rid myself of the horrible shame that was eating at my mind like a caustic acid.

Usually the name of the church caught my attention. After so many rejections I started to judge churches by their denominations. It hurts me to say this but in all my years of living as a transient homeless man who was not always clean-shaven and wearing nice clothes, people who said they loved God had a bad habit of making snap judgments by appearance. When a person comes to church they are looking for some sort of spiritual help. It may only be a comfortable feeling that comes from going to church. Even if it is only to appease your conscience, people go to church for a reason; they want comfort. I have sat so many times in the back of a church watching people stare at me. The turn their heads and whisper one to another and then at the end of the service walk right past me as though I did not exist. Many men who stood in pulpits and preached the sermons were curt with me as they rushed me through their obligatory politeness. As they gave me a brush off, I was made to feel so insignificant. All I ever wanted was the God I saw in Bob's eyes but I never found him. What I did find was men and women sitting in their nice suits and dresses, driving their fine cars, sitting in their pews at the front half of the church, leaving me to sit alone at the back of a church. And if ever I felt like sitting closer to the people sitting in the front, they would move away or an usher would ask me to sit at the back of a church.

What I did find was judgment. Where did I find acceptance? On the streets with the homeless in the inner city. But even there I was a loner. I would spend many hours per day sitting in libraries. I could not take the books out of the library because I did not have a fixed address. So I sat and read. I was looking for an escape from my own inner prison that drugs and alcohol would not remove. I searched through books on philosophy, psychology, sociology, anthropology, metaphysics, occult, and theology. Year after year I accumulated knowledge. I guess you could say I have a Ph.D. from Hobo U. For all the finger pointing that the homeless receive from people who think they understand homelessness, I say to you: I have lived with homeless men and women for enough years that I can safely say there is not a greater group of people who understand what community means than we the people who society tries to ignore. I have lived from coast to coast and wherever I find another person who lives on the streets, I have found a friend.

There is also a code of behavior for things that are accepted and things that are not. To cross the line is to find yourself on the receiving end of anger and judgment that can be swift, sure and painful. It is a place where the weak fall fast, if not physically at least emotionally. Churches all over the country use the homeless to appease their conscience. I call them Saturday afternoon Christians. They come to the inner city once a month and pass out some tracts and give you patronizing platitudes and nothing more. "God bless you, stay warm," they say as they leave you cold and hungry. For God and for love, it is a sad reality that I have seen.

The next town I hitchhiked to was Vancouver. I lived on Main Street, near East Hastings, and on Granville Street. I used to wander for hours, lost in shame. I found myself in New West Minister where I found a church. It was a Pentecostal Church. This church was a rarity. They seemed to offer a glimpse of the God Bob had shown me. The preacher preached as though the word he used from the Bible was alive inside of him. I was awestruck. I had never heard a man speak like this man. He knew nothing of the wrongs that had been done to me, and one day he started to preach about the wrongs of homosexual behavior. He said homosexual behavior was hated by God. I took that to mean I was a terrible and worthless man. Now I knew I could never tell a soul of the acts that Jack did to me. And on top of that, I started to feel hopeless. I still wanted to find God but it was becoming increasingly difficult to believe God loved me.

On April 1, 1981, I called my sister just to say hello. We lived in the same town but we saw each other very little. I remember her words as though I just heard them today. "Oh, my god, Nobody, I forgot about you. Dad is not expected to last through tonight. We are going home to see him before he dies."

Thunder struck my heart. I put the phone on the receiver and in a dazed state I called the minister. Tearfully I told him my problem, that my dad was going to die and I could not get home. To my amazement the church sent me home on the plane that same day.

When I got to Kelowna I went straight to the Kelowna General Hospital and saw my father with tubes in his body. He was in a coma unaware that I was there. I had only seen my dad a few times since I left home and our relationship was strained. I know that he loved me but what was he to do with his son that had caused him so much heartache and who now lived on the streets so far below his potential. Every time I saw my father I felt so much shame, I never told him what had happened to me. After I saw him, my brothers, sisters, my mother and I went home to toss and turn through a restless night.

Early in the morning we were back at the hospital. We saw Dad for a few minutes and then the nurses had to take care of him. They told us to come back in about twenty minutes. We all left and went down to the cafeteria. About a half-hour later we came back to see the nurses rushing in and out of his room. It was obvious something was wrong. My fears came true when a nurse came out of the room to inform us that my father had passed away. At that very moment I felt like the top of my head opened and someone poured a load of heavy sand through my body, and then I went numb. I walked to a pay phone and made a phone call, and then I went back into my father's room and watched his lifeless body. I held his hand and when the nurses came in to prepare his body to go to the morgue I finally left.

When I was sixteen I wanted to go home. I wanted to find myself back in my own bed. I wanted to go to school. I wanted to stop my addiction but instead I got destroyed in my heart, in my mind, and in my life and I lost the last four years of my father's life.

When I got back to New West Minister, life for me became even more dysfunctional. I started to drink with vengeance. I remember drinking one Sunday with an old wino and a hooker who was about forty. At about six-thirty that night these two friends and I polished of a four-litre bottle of red wine. I decided I was going to go to church. I was so drunk I could barely stand but in my stupor, I felt ten feet tall and bulletproof as I stumbled into church. I had the old wino's hat on my head. It was dirty and smelled really bad. I sat on the back pew through the whole service. I sat and mumbled incoherent drivel about nothing important. I think I was disrupting the service.

For those who are not familiar with the order of a Pentecostal service it can be put into three categorical stages. There is the song service where songs of worship and praise are sung. Then there is the sermon and the last stage is called the altar call, where men and women who want prayer, or who want to pray, can go to the front of the church. This is a very reverential part of the service. It was at this point that I stumbled out of my pew and made my way to the front of the church. Not to pray but to utter threatening words to someone I was mad at. The church ushers led me out of the church and sent me home but not before I breathed out even more threatening words.

It was Monday morning when the pastor called me into his office. He told me that I should leave the church and not come back. I felt the shame for what Jack had done to me, and it turned to anger and now the anger was turning into rage. The object of my rage was whomever I decided I was going to be mad at. Nothing was as important to me now. I left New Westminster and hitchhiked east running from everyone, including me.

I was becoming very antisocial. I hated people but I hated myself even more than I hated people. I buried my hate beneath a cloak of emotional silence, no one knew how I felt. I became a chameleon. I made myself adaptable to whatever environment I found myself.

A sad side effect was I lost touch with who I was more and more. This is a dangerous place to find yourself in. I became lost in a desolate place where so many homeless people find themselves. In an emotional oblivion, being disenfranchised and marginalized. I wandered back into the interior of BC. When I stopped I was in Salmon Arm, I met four friends. They allowed me to sleep on the floor of the basement apartment they rented. The house was out in the country. I stayed with them for about one month. It was here I met Sally who became the mother of my son Sam, my son of whom I have always been proud. I first met Sally at another one of those church meetings that I always found myself at.

One day my friends and I were going back to the house where we all stayed. We had gone into town earlier. As we passed by this huge ranch I saw a lot of men, women and children walking around dressed like they were going to church. I asked one of my friends who these people were. The response to my question was the wrong answer to give me. They said, "They are a cult. You should stay away," which settled the question for me. I was going to investigate.

I hopped on a bike and rode to the farm to check out these people. As I rode onto the property, heads turned to see me. There was a quizzical look in a lot of the eyes. As I put my bike down I started to look around. I was full of curiosity. Who are these people? Was the question in my mind.

In a few minutes a couple of men started to approach me. When they reached me they introduced themselves. They introduced themselves as brothers. They were referred to as *the Friends* by others they told me, or they are called the *Two by Twos* because they go out into the mission field two at a time. All these people were there for a meeting and if I wanted I could join them. I was always looking for the God I had seen in Bob's eyes. I thought I might find him here.

As the meeting progressed I found myself being very bored by lots of dry information being droned out of the mouth of men who looked like they were speaking from a torture chamber instead of from a book that offered life and hope. The songs they sung sounded like a funeral dirge. What they did have that was very impressive to me was that they were very organized. There were about six hundred people at this meeting. They fed everyone three times a day; it took three hours, I think, between two meetings. All these people were fed in two sittings, and all the dishes were washed, and the volunteers were back in place for the next meeting.

It was between the meetings that I met a girl. We

started to hang around together. By the second day her parents thought I was too unsavory for their daughter to get too close to. They got another person to sit between us during the services. The girl was eighteen and I was twenty-one. We quickly became friends. Her name was Sally and more than twenty-five years later, we are still friends. I met her sisters and brothers and her mom and dad. For the rest of the convention we sat together and talked between meetings. When the weekend was over, she told me how to get to her place and she went back to her home. I started to feel that alone feeling again. Sally had become too close to me and raised way too many fears that I did not like, so I did what I knew to do best whenever these feelings started to rise to what I felt was an uncomfortable feeling. I packed my bag and hitchhiked across Canada.

The end of July and the first week of August in 1983 I was traveling along the Trans Canada Highway. One pleasure I have had repeatedly over the past twenty-five years is seeing this great country that has been my home. The geography is so unique from the West Coast to the East Coast. The mountains, the interior, the Rocky Mountains all lead into the foothills and these are only the gateway to the prairies. After seeing flat land for days you are led to the Canadian shield as the highway winds around the Great Lakes. You are allowed to view scenery that will fill your mind with awe through Ontario and into the Laurentians and then outward into the East Coast. I have met thousands of people over the many years that I traveled. You can see the regional mind-set of people as you travel. I can proudly say I love Canada, the true north strong and free. I have called seventy different communities my home over all these years.

On this journey I was heading to Macadam, New Brunswick. This small town on the East Coast was my first experience where the police station closed at eight o'clock and was closed on weekends. While I was there I could not get Sally out of my mind. So after two weeks I headed back to Enderby, BC.

Let me help you with a little math. In about one month that year, I traveled by thumb approximately six thousand miles. In all my years of travel I made it back to the west in the fastest time I ever have. On that trip it only took me four days and twenty-three hours.

I got to the country road that led to Sally's place, which seemed like it was in the middle of nowhere. I walked down a private road surrounded by fields of hay and these fields were surrounded by forests. I walked up to a house that was partly made of bails of hay and logs. I walked up some stairs to hear a girl singing. It was Sally. She came to the door in blue jeans, a plaid shirt and rubber boots. Not the girl I saw wearing a dress all through the weekend meeting. This was the beginning of a romantic relationship that lasted until December of 1985 when Sally and I could no longer live together: I was not a nice man. My inner demons of guilt and shame had driven me into a state of slow, simmering rage that left me emotionally closed down.

Six months prior to Sally and I ending our dysfunctional relationship, she gave birth to Sam on June 2, 1985. I was the first man, other than the doctor, to hold my son in my arms; a day I will never forget. I left Sally and went to Kamloops; my drug addiction was out of control. I was getting used to failure. Since 1978 my interpersonal skills were becoming more and more dysfunctional. I truly despised myself and I did not trust anyone, but at the same time, I maintained a certain sense of behavior on the streets that would not betray this inner hatred I held so deep in my heart. As a result, I became more and more antisocial. The roots of my diagnosis can be traced to this period of time. I had a borderline personality disorder.

I was only in Kamloops for a short period of time when I hitchhiked back to Vancouver. I lived on a cot in the back of a soup kitchen on Main Street. It was here that I befriended a man whose name was John. He was an inner city man who had spent many years in the BC penitentiary and now his life was spent drinking, cooking wine, popping pills and living on the streets. We were friends although I never drank with John; we would spend hours talking.

One day I saw him stumbling down the street holding his pants around his waist. He had been so badly beaten he had emptied his bowels. He was too beaten and sick to care for himself. So at the back of a Christian mission I cleaned up my friend. It was too much for him. The next time I saw him, which was a couple of days later, he was sitting on a curbside drifting into unconsciousness. I found an empty prescription bottle in his shirt. He was trying to die. I called an ambulance. He was treated and let go. Let go to what? Back to the streets, a lonely place. Unless you have lived there, you will not understand. Rooming houses, shelters, back alleys and parks, soup kitchens, garbage cans begging and disdain from those who do not understand but who love to judge. I will close this part of my book with two poems:

# MY NAME IS NOBODY

Let me tell you of a place that exists
In so many cities and towns;
The city may change in location
And size but this place exists.
Most people try to turn their eyes,

And say it does not exist.
This place? It is the place of the homeless.
Who am I?
And what gives me the right to say that most people
Try to say it does not exist?
My name is Nobody
I heard a mother say in response to her child's enquiry
"Mommy, who is that man?"
As she pointed toward me
"Nobody, dear, he is a homeless man."

# YOU PASS ME BY

When you pass me by I hear you say, "He is so dirty
how can he live that way?"
I ask you to stop and think, why are you so callous?
Do you know what brought me here?
To the curb of the street where I sit as you pass me by.
I was beaten by life once, got up brushed off the dust
only to be beaten again.
I went numb, and no longer felt the pain, life became
empty meaningless and vain.
And here I sit as you pass me by you never hear my
silent cry, and you never see my
invisible tear, but here I sit year after year and yet
you stare as you pass me by.
What's the use, why even try?
Well I lost my mind...

I became very adept at hiding my pain. Those incessant
voices of guilt, and shame that whispered their cries into
the depths of my heart, and the anger and rage that
pounded screams into my inner ear. I learned to hide
from them all. How did I hide? I buried them, under a

ferocious search for knowledge. Wherever I was, whatever city or town I was in, I always found a library and there I would search the shelves for information, it was an obsession. I read about seven subjects; whatever I could find on philosophy, psychology, sociology, anthropology, metaphysics, occult and theology. For twenty-five years, these were my studies every winter, spring, summer and fall, from Vancouver to Charlottetown. The more I learned, the more tormented I became. I did, on the other hand, acquire an education that you cannot buy.

It was 1993 in February. I could no longer hide from my pain. I can remember the day very clearly. I was talking to some friends when all of a sudden I felt as though someone had opened a crater in the deepest part of my mind; it was the pit in an abyss. The abyss of a nervous breakdown, the crater opened and I fell into that abyss. My friends had no idea what had just occurred inside of my mind, but that day is a memory that will always stay with me. There was no longer enough alcohol or drugs to take away my grief. Neither were there enough books that I could run to.

It was the middle of March, when I was in my 1989, Datsun B2-10 it was brown and full of rust, I only paid two hundred dollars for. I started to drive. First I headed from Kelowna up the highway toward Prince George. The only thought that I had was: I want to die. It became a very confusing and dangerous emotion. I wanted to die and end my inner pain but at the same time I was afraid of what I would face on the other side of death. Sometimes I could no longer resist the desire and I did not care about the other side of death.

# DEATH

I have stood at death's door and knocked
I have screamed come and take me
I have knocked four different times
Come and take me!
No answer
My eyes open my thoughts are groggy
There is a stabbing in my right wrist
Intravenous...
You cannot drip hope into a broken heart
I have stood at death's door four times
Come and take me!
No answer

I wanted to end this pain. I had driven for about a day. I was on the Alaska Highway between Dawson Creek and Taylor, on a lonely stretch of the highway. I was coming toward a logging truck, and as calm as if I was walking on a sandy beach with the cool breeze blowing across my face, I pulled my car into the oncoming lane straight toward a fully loaded logging truck. I gripped the steering wheel and with an emotionless face I prepared to die, smashing into tons of metal and logs heading toward me at sixty miles an hour. I can only imagine the fear that must have instantly entered the mind of the trucker as he saw this small Datsun coming at him. He must have known he would drive right over me. His lights started to flash frantically. As calmly as I entered his lane at the last minute, I turned back into my own, and kept driving, as though nothing had happened.

I was coming apart emotionally and mentally. I was driving toward my brother's house about fifty miles north of Dawson Creek, BC, but my mind was so confused and unsettled, that I changed my mind. I could not think of what I could tell my brother about why I was showing up at his house eight hundred miles from where I lived. I turned my car around and started to head toward Alberta. I was going to drive across Canada.

On March 24, 1993, I was in Lethbridge, Alberta. It was my thirty-first birthday and loneliness was all I knew in my heart. In a deep and painful way I realized I was alone. My twin sister was in Calgary, with my mother and other brothers and sisters; they had no idea where I was. They did not know where I was in my physical location and they had no idea where I was mentally or emotionally.

In Lethbridge I found a restaurant that gave you a free dinner if it was your birthday. So for my birthday dinner, I had bacon and eggs, easy over, with a double order of brown toast and a large glass of milk with a coffee. For dessert I had a piece of apple pie with cheese melted on the top. It tasted so good. When I finished my dinner I got back into my car and kept driving east. I had no idea where I was going but looking back, having many years between that day and today, and as I am writing these words to consider things, I can understand what I was doing. I was trying to escape from something I could no longer handle.

In 1978, I was sixteen years old, according to the law of the land I was still considered a child, and emotionally, I most definitely was a child. Sexual abuse happens to a child when an adult uses a child for sexual purposes. Children are not able to give informed consent to sexual activity because they cannot fully understand the adult sexual contract or predict the consequences. The adult abuses their authority over the child. It is one of the most painful and damaging experiences a child can suffer. It was this pain I was trying to run from. It was this pain that drove me since the first day Jack violated my innocence.

When I was driving somewhere on the prairies late on the second day, the muffler of my car fell off and started to drag along the highway. I had to remove it before I went any farther. But I had a problem. If I turned off my car I would not be able to start it again, because I was having problems with the starter. I had to jump-start the car. My problem was the prairies are flat, and I would be unable to jump-start the car. What did I do? I stopped the car and while the car was still running I blocked the back wheel then I crawled underneath the car while on the Trans Canada and with my bare hands I pulled the muffler off. When I got back in the car I could not hear the radio because of the sound of the rumbling from a manifold without a tail pipe. I drove continuously four days in a row stopping only for roadside naps and gas.

When I got to Thunder Bay, my car could only muster about thirty miles an hour; that was the top speed. As my car finally broke down and could no longer go on, an ironic thing happened. I broke down too and couldn't go any further either. As my habit had been, I found the local shelter for the homeless and I registered to stay but my mind was racing too fast with uncontrollable thoughts. When your mind can no longer cope with the thoughts emotions and memories of a traumatic experience it starts to act in a dysfunctional way. I was confused scared and alone. I started to weep.Tears fell down my cheeks like a river. My pain was releasing its fury and I could not stop it. I got in my car and inched along the street at snail's pace.

I drove to the hospital, parked my car at the front of the building and went in. When the crisis nurse finally came to see me I was an emotional mess. As soon as I started to talk it was with a painful, crying voice. She sat and listened and at intervals she would ask another question and I would bawl even more to her; it was obvious I was in crisis. For the first time in ten years I started to talk. I did not really make sense. My words at first were as fast as my thoughts and I am sure just as mixed up. It was obvious that I had not conformed to the social norm of society for many years.

I was admitted into Lake-Head psychiatric hospital in March of 1993. I was there for almost one month. And it was here that I was given the diagnosis of sociopath tendencies. How did they determine this diagnosis? By giving me a psychological test, and by the psychiatrist, talking with me. What they failed to find out was the reason why I failed to conform. But I can not totally lay the reason they did not know on them because I only talked around the real issues. I was admitted into the hospital and was there for about one month.

It was the start of a seven-year journey that was more painful for me than all the years I was a homeless man. I left the hospital still confused but now I was medicated. The hospital would not release me until I had a place to go. What a conundrum. A homeless man, not able to leave the hospital, without an address. That is how I ended up at a recovery house in Thunder Bay. Life unraveled at this point. I know that sounds strange having read my story to this point. I am sure you are thinking: "Starting to unravel? It sounds like it already has." It now became completely unbearable.

The cry for help was louder in my head. I did not want this inner pain, neither did I want to hide from it any more. There is a diagnosis in the Diagnostic and Statistical Manual of Mental Disorders called suicidal ideation. This is a fancy word that refers to the constant and obsessive desire to die with plans and attempts filling your thoughts. Not caring if you die, in hindsight, is the worst place I have ever been. I have had so much charcoal pumped into my body I sometimes think maybe my blood has turned black as the charcoal. I remember one time standing on the edge of a bridge. I climbed over the railing. My mind went into a haze as all that happened to me played through my mind. I was convinced that life was a useless existence. I was about to let go and drop to the freeway below, when a police officer grabbed my hand.

Another time when the grief was more than I could bear, I took all the lithium pills I had saved up. There were over one hundred. Each pill was five hundred milligrams. I was living in a group home (a hellish experience all by itself). I took all the medication I had, walked into the living room, sat on the couch, closed my eyes in silence, and prepared to die. I went unconscious. I don't know for how long but when I came to consciousness I was in the hospital's intensive care unit. My arm had an IV in it. Years later I calculated the approximate amount of lithium in my body; it was over seven hundred thousand milligrams. Four times I awoke in intensive care when other suicidal attempts had failed.

A person that is diagnosed as having a bipolar disorder swings from a high-spirited state of thinking, causing behavior to become grandiose, then becoming extremely depressed where hope is a dark pit of great distress. This was a mental state I had to deal with. This a horrible existence. One day I could laugh and talk, and the next day all I could do was cry. Confusion was my way of life.

In another group home where I lived my antisocial behavior was very evident. I was very aggressive in my actions and in my words. Another male resident in the group home and I had been exchanging words for days when I finally pushed him to the point of throwing a punch. He hit me so hard my eyes went black for a split second. Two days later I had five grand mal seizures. This sent me into a coma for four days. I had a brain hemorrhage. Life was truly now completely unbearable.

When I lived in another group home in Newmarket, Ontario, I proceeded to pursue a civil law suit against Jack and the Christian shelter. My lawyer required all my psychiatric records from all my hospital stays. The insurance company for the Christian shelter requested these records. My lawyer gave me a copy of each of the records when he got them. There were six or seven thick books from several of the hospitals I had been in. It was what was in these medical records that became the catalyst for my burning desire not to end up as another statistic.

When I left Newmarket I ended up in a town called Jackson Point, Ontario. My behavior was very uncontrollable and for that reason not very many group homes wanted me around but one home took the tough cases, so to speak. It was here in 1999.That I started to read these hospital reports. Let me paint you a picture. I am a man who has a shattered lifestyle, with an unstable emotional constitution, who was medicated almost into incoherence. Every day I would take 1500 mg of lithium 60 mg of paxil 900 mg of dilantin 1.5 mg of clomzapam and 250 mg of Trazidone, at bedtime. I was on so much medication that my speech was slurred and I staggered like I was drunk. It was in this condition that I started to read the hospital reports. I became obsessed with everything that was written about me.

The first time I read through them, it was all jargon to me. The second time I read through them I saw a pattern. When I saw this pattern I was incensed. The pattern that I saw was this: one doctor or hospital staff would write what their assessment was of my condition. When I changed towns or doctors the reports would follow and all other reports that followed were read with a bias that was accepted as truth. The treatment would proceed along a preconceived bias so no one was taking the time or the effort, to find out what was the root cause of my mental and emotional dilemmas. I decided one time to count all the different psychological assessments that were made on me, the reasons why I was the way I was. I counted twenty-two different psychological diagnoses from the D.S.M. I went into a very deep blackness mentally; this was too much for my fragile mind.

These were the people who were to offer me some kind of hope. They had written into the report that there was little hope that I would ever leave the transient lifestyle, and it was their evaluation that I would find myself in and out of institutions for a long period of time. It was coming up to the new millennium so I decided that this was the end of all this broken merry-go-round. I was not going to be a statistic. I was not going to spend my life like this anymore. I had what some would call an epiphany. It was a very poignant moment in my life. I planned what I was going to do in my mental and emotional haze with my life as shattered as it was, there was only one thing I could do.

New Year's Eve, 1999, was a very solemn day for me. I was anxious for the millennium to roll across the skies of Ontario. Across the street from the group home where I lived was Lake Simcoe. It was frozen. The ice was covered with a crust of snow. At 11:30 p.m. I walked out onto the lake and sat. With a sense of solemnity I contemplated thirty-eight years of my life.

As the millennium came into existence with all the inner pomp and pageantry that I could muster, I took a very deep breath, stood to my feet, looked up at the stars and exhaled. I told myself: I am coming back from this hell. With another deliberate choice I put one foot in front of the other and started to walk. This was my own little ceremony, I gave myself a new point of reference. I had no idea how I was going to accomplish what I was planning to do. All I knew was it was time to do it.

# FREEDOM IS NOT JUST ANOTHER WORD

I woke up on January, 1, 2000, and although I had to take my medication, for the first time since I was sixteen I felt as though I had my life in my hands. I knew I was very ill. There were no delusions for me where that is concerned. I knew that I had been horribly wronged by a sexual deviant. I had examined my entire life and I knew it to be completely broken. But on this first day of a new millennium I had a hope ringing in my heart. Was there an instant change in my life? No. Far from it, but hope is a very powerful fuel.

I left Jackson Point. I traveled for Prince Edward Island. I wanted to trace my family tree. My mother was a Hickey before she married my father. While I was there I was still struggling with a lot of emotions that I was not able to control, but I was working toward that end, to regain my heart. Back in Kelowna, my son was fourteen years old. I had come to understand that he was having troubles in his personal life. I was afraid he was going to become a street kid, I did not want that for him. I wanted more for him than that. I got on a Greyhound bus and rode for ninety hours until I got to Kelowna.

It was a trip I almost could not endure. I was still not emotionally strong when I got to Kelowna. The first place I went was to the hospital where I was admitted, and after about two weeks, the hospital put me into a group home. Anger is never an easy emotion to take control of especially when it has had free reign for so many years.

My anger got me into trouble again. I found myself locked inside a small room on the psychiatric ward, with a doctor threatening to send me to a forensic psychiatric hospital near Vancouver. I pleaded with this man for nine days while I remained locked in this small room. I was under twenty-four hour surveillance. The doctor finally decided he was not going to send me to the forensic hospital and I was released to another group home. But now I had a charge of uttering threats to do death or bodily harm. When I read the accusations of those who accused me of the threats, I knew that ninety percent of what was said about me was a lie.

For about three months I lived in the new group home. I continued to work hard on the issues that had kept me so bound and broken for twenty-five years as a homeless man. I had enough of the entire mental health system. I left the group home. I stepped back into the ranks of the homeless. When I lived on the street I had a street name. The name people called me was Merlin. I had a good reputation on the streets with this name. While staying in a shelter in Kelowna a friend by the name of Raven came to me. He told me that he was starting a squat to protest the problems that were obvious between the homeless and the shelter. He told me he was calling it Camp Freedom. We made our homestead/squat in an abandoned lot on Richter Street. It was during this time that I stopped taking all my medications. I decided that if the doctors wanted to assign me to a prognosis of being a long-term patient of the psychiatric system that I was the only one who could help me.

Since New Year's Day of 2000, I had been thinking about all my years of reading about psychology, philosophy, and theology. In a little bit at a time, I had put together a hypothesis. It was time for me to implement my hypothesis. I had nothing to lose and everything to gain. I also decided I would not tell anyone what I had done. My father was an avid golfer and whenever he had a task that was important to him he would say: keep your head down and follow through with your swing. With quiet determination I did just that. The main reason for this was the fact that I was court ordered to see a psychiatrist and that I was court ordered to take my medication. So in November of 2001, I stopped taking three thousand milligrams of medication and implemented my hypothesis. And in the process of doing this I found my freedom and now you see why freedom for me is not just another word, it is a reality that I live daily.

CPSIA information can be obtained at www.ICGtesting.com
230024LV00008B/322/P

9 781424 181674